# 抗击冰雪
# 心系人民

## 新闻摄影展作品集

中华全国新闻工作者协会
中国新闻摄影学会

# Braving the Snowstorm

All-China Journalists' Association
The Photojournalist Society of China

人民美術出版社

只要紧紧依靠广大人民群众,充分发挥社会主义制度能够集中力量办大事的政治优势,我们就一定能够战胜前进道路上的各种挑战和风险,不断把中国特色社会主义伟大事业推向前进。

——摘自《中国共产党第十七届中央委员会第二次全休会议公报》

We are certainly able to overcome various risks and challenges on the road ahead, and constantly push forward the great cause of building socialism with Chinese characteristics, as long as we closely rely on the broad masses of the people, while giving full play to the advantages of socialist political system in concentrating forces on major tasks.

——Excerpt from the communique issued by the Second Plenary Session of the 17th Central Committee of the Communist Party of China

要大力宣传这次抗灾救灾斗争中涌现出来的模范人物和先进事迹,进一步激发全党全国各族人民为改革开放和社会主义现代化建设而团结奋斗的热情。

——摘自《中国共产党第十七届中央委员会第二次全体会议公报》

We should vigorously publicize the advanced models and deeds emerged from the struggle of the disaster relief so as to further inspire the enthusiasm of the whole Party and the people of all ethnic groups on striving for the process of reform, opening-up and socialist modernization drive.

——Excerpt from the communique issued by the Second Plenary Session of the 17th Central Committee of the Communist Party of China

# 前　言

## Foreword

　　2008年初，我国南方一些地区遭受了严重的低温雨雪冰冻灾害。党中央、国务院高度重视、周密部署，各有关部门紧急行动、全力以赴，全国军民众志成城、奋勇抗灾。广大新闻工作者顶风冒雪、深入一线，积极投身到抗灾救灾宣传报道之中。他们以皑皑白雪为纸，以激情热血为墨，以摄影镜头为眼，真实记录下了这段战天斗地的英雄画卷！

　　In early 2008, snow-related disasters struck many provinces and regions in southern China. CPC Central Committee and State leaders spared no effort to help the masses and work out series of relief plans. The nation rallied together to fight the snow and sleet disaster and help their fellow countrymen and women. Reporters and photographers were on the frontline, braving the hardship and fighting fatigue. Using the snow as a canvas and their cameras as brushes, they painted the real scenes and recorded the heart-breaking events in the snow-ravaged provinces.

# 编 辑 委 员 会

# 情系于民

## Nourishing Affection for the People

真情融冰雪，抗灾党旗红。面对紧急灾情，党和国家领导人心系灾区人民，运筹帷幄，亲临一线，坐镇指挥，鼓舞了广大军民抗灾救灾的昂扬斗志，增强了必胜信心。

The snow crisis has been solved as the result of the joint effort of the leadership of the Party and the whole society. The State leaders visited storm-hit areas to supervise and expedite relief work. Their leadership encouraged the masses and warmed the hearts of people in the snow-ravaged provinces.

2008年2月5日至6日，中共中央总书记、国家主席、中央军委主席胡锦涛来到广西桂林市考察抗灾救灾工作。这是胡锦涛在资源县中峰乡八坊村竹子水屯看望受灾村民。　　新华社／鞠　鹏

Chinese President Hu Jintao visits villagers in Ziyuan county, Guilin city, Guangxi Zhuang autonomous region, on February 6, 2008. Hu inspected the relief work operations and visited locals suffering from the snowstorms.　Xinhua / Ju Peng

2008年2月5日至6日，中共中央总书记、国家主席、中央军委主席胡锦涛来到广西桂林市考察抗灾救灾工作。这是胡锦涛同正在执行救灾任务的广州军区某集团军陆航团的官兵一起装运救灾物资。　新华社发

President Hu Jintao takes a hands-on role helping soldiers to dispatch disaster-relief materials at an airport in Guangxi Zhuang autonomous region. Hu also visited local communities during the first three days of the Spring Festival holidays.　Xinhua

2008 年 2 月 3 日，受胡锦涛总书记委托，中共中央政治局常委、全国人大常委会委员长吴邦国专程到国家电网公司、铁道部调度指挥中心和北京西站，代表党中央、国务院，向奋战在抢险抗灾一线的电力、铁路系统广大干部职工表示亲切慰问。这是吴邦国在北京西站候车室与旅客亲切攀谈。　　新华社/李　涛

Wu Bangguo (R), chairman of the Standing Committee of the National People's Congress (NPC), talks to passengers at the Beijing West Railway Station, on February 3, 2008. 　Xinhua / Li Tao

抗击冰雪 心系人民
Braving the Snowstorm

2008年1月29日，中共中央政治局常委、国务院总理温家宝在湖南长沙火车站看望滞留车站的旅客。温家宝总理对旅客说："春节快到了，我给大家拜个早年！你们被困在火车站，还没能提早回家，我表示深深的歉意，现在我们正在想尽一切办法抢修，一定把大家送回家过春节。" 新华社／姚大伟

Chinese Premier Wen Jiabao uses a loudspeaker to encourage the stranded passengers at the Changsha Railway Station in Hunan province on January 29, 2008. Wen apologizes for the delay of the trains and wishes the stranded people a happy Spring Festival. Xinhua / Yao Dawei

2008年1月30日至2月1日，受胡锦涛总书记委托，中共中央政治局常委、全国政协主席贾庆林来到安徽合肥、六安等受灾严重的地区，深入火车站、汽车站、供电公司、农产品批发市场、蔬菜生产基地、敬老院和农户家中，实地察看工农业受损和群众受灾情况，慰问奋战在抗灾救灾第一线的广大干部群众和人民解放军、武警部队官兵、公安民警。这是1月31日，贾庆林在六安市舒城县桃溪镇慰问受灾的村民。

新华社／刘卫兵

Jia Qinglin (L), member of the Standing Committee of the Political Bureau of the Communist Party of China (CPC) Central Committee, shakes hands with an elderly villager in Taoxi town, Liuan city, Anhui province, on January 31, 2008. On behalf of the Central Committee of the CPC and the State Council, Jia visited the snow-hit Anhui province from January 30 to February 1 to boost the morale of snow fighters and guide relief work.

Xinhua / Liu Weibing

受胡锦涛总书记委托，中共中央政治局常委李长春专程赴湖北灾区，代表党中央、国务院慰问受灾群众，考察指导抗灾救灾工作。这是 2008 年 1 月 31 日，李长春在湖北武汉金口街蔬菜基地视察蔬菜受灾情况。

新华社／刘建生

Li Changchun (front L), (member of the Standing Committee of the Political Bureau of the Communist Party of China (CPC) Central Committee), talks with farmers during his visit at a vegetable production base in Hubei province, on January 31, 2008. Entrusted by CPC Central Committee General Secretary Hu Jintao, Li visited Hubei province to meet the people suffering from the snowstorm and inspected disaster relief work on behalf of the CPC Central Committee and the State Council.

Xinhua / Liu Jiansheng

受胡锦涛总书记委托，中共中央政治局常委、中央书记处书记习近平于 2008 年 1 月 30 日至 2 月 1 日专程赶赴贵州，代表党中央、国务院慰问受灾群众，指导抗灾救灾工作。这是 1 月 31 日，习近平来到贵州省铜仁地区玉屏县万山特区高楼坪乡老山口村受灾的侗族村民唐召维（左一）家慰问。　　新华社／兰红光

Xi Jinping (C), member of the Standing Committee of the Political Bureau of the Communist Party of China (CPC) Central Committee, visits the family of Tang Zhaowei (L) of the Dong ethnic group at Gaolouping town in Yuping county, Guizhou province, on January 31, 2008. Xi Jinping was in Guizhou deploying relief work and consoling residents suffering from snowstorm.

Xinhua / Lan Hongguang

抗击冰雪　心系人民
Braving the Snowstorm

受胡锦涛总书记委托，中共中央政治局常委李克强于
2008年1月30日至2月2日专程奔赴四川灾区，察看
灾情，代表党中央、国务院看望慰问受灾群众，指导
抗灾救灾工作。这是2月1日，李克强在邻水县城北镇
罗解村察看蔬菜受灾情况。　　　　新华社／李学仁

Li Keqiang (2nd L), member of the Standing Committee of the Political Bureau of the Communist
Party of China (CPC) Central Committee, inspects
ruined vegetable crops in Chengbei town of Linshui
county, Sichuan province, on February 1, 2008.
Entrusted by CPC Central Committee General Secretary Hu Jintao, Li Keqiang visited Sichuan from
January 30 to February 2 to meet people suffering
from the snowstorm and inspect disaster relief
work on behalf of the CPC Central Committee and
the State Council.　Xinhua / Li Xueren

受胡锦涛总书记委托，中共中央政治局常委、中央纪委书记贺国强代表党中央、国务院，来到江西省察看雨雪冰冻灾害情况，慰问灾区干部群众，与省委、省政府一道研究指导抗灾救灾工作。这是 2008 年 1 月 31 日，贺国强踏着湿滑冰雪，沿着陡峭山路实地察看九江市庐山区莲花镇妙智村220千伏输电线路抢修现场。
新华社／黄敬文

He Guoqiang (Front L), member of the Standing Committee of the Political Bureau of the Communist Party of China (CPC) Central Committee, inspects the repair operations at an electric power station in Lianhua town of Jiujiang city, Jiangxi province, on January 31, 2008. He later helped direct disaster relief work and console local residents suffering from snowstorm.
Xinhua / Huang Jingwen

受胡锦涛总书记委托，中共中央政治局常委、中央政法委书记、国务委员周永康奔赴河南雨雪冰冻灾区，代表党中央、国务院看望慰问受灾群众和奋战在抗灾救灾一线的干部群众，实地察看灾情，指导抗灾救灾工作。这是2月1日到达后的当天深夜，周永康深入救灾第一线慰问河南路政、公安人员。　新华社／饶爱民

Zhou Yongkang (R), member of the Standing Committee of the Political Bureau of the Communist Party of China (CPC) Central Committee, shakes hands with a road worker in Henan province, on February 1, 2008. Zhou praised Henan for its contributions to disaster relief in other parts of the country by opening all entrances and exits on expressways in the province and providing support to transit vehicles.　Xinhua / Rao Aimin

2008 年 2 月 5 日 12 时许，在北京飞往贵阳的飞机上，
记者航拍到贵州省部分遭受雪凝灾害地区的奇特景象。
中国日报／徐京星

Snow-covered mountains in Guizhou province, on
February 5, 2008.    China Daily／Xu Jingxing

## 第二部分

# 奋起抗灾

## Braving the Storm

灾情就是命令，灾区就是战场。无论是千里大救援、京珠大破冰，还是滞车大分流、雪地大保电，广大干部群众冲上去了，解放军和武警官兵冲上去了，筑起了抗击冰雪的钢铁长城。

The disaster region was a battle-field and the mission was to restore order. PLA soldiers and police officers rushed to the frontlines to rescue stranded travelers, clear frozen expressways, direct stranded vehicles and repair transmission towers. They were fuelled by a passion to help and got the job done by using their shoulders, legs and bare hands.

受冰冻天气影响,江西省龙南县偏远山村灾情
严重,村民生活十分困难,龙南县迅速组织人
员解救受困村民。图为2月3日,一名工作人
员将80岁老人陈章德背出受困的金莲村。至
当日下午,1761位受困村民被成功解救。
赣南日报／赖锦洪

A rescuer carries Chen Zhangde, an 80-
year-old woman, to safety out of Jinlian
village in Longnan county, Jiangxi province,
on February 3, 2008. Some 1,761 people
in the village were trapped for days in
freezing conditions without electricity and
water. All were rescued.

Gannan Daily / Lai Jinhong

这是京珠高速韶关段滞留的车辆，他们已在冰天雪地里待了三天。

南方日报／曾　强

Motorists were stranded for three days on the ice-covered Shaoguan section of the expressway from Beijing to Zhuhai.

Nanfang Daily / Zeng Qiang

在南京火车站送站坪上，一位车站派出所的民警在暴雪中
喊哑了嗓子，湿透了衣服。　东方卫报／朱　格

A policeman helps guide stranded train travelers at
the Nanjing Railway Station, Jiangsu province.
Orient Guardian / Zhu Ge

广州军区某部装甲分队正在为灾区执行特殊输送任务。 广东75200 部队政治部宣传处／覃明章

An armored vehicle from a military base in Guangdong province transports relief materials to snow-trapped residents.
Guangdong No.75200 Troop / Qin Mingzhang

1月23日，消防官兵在长沙市楚湘街社区长沙港老宿舍除冰。
三湘都市报／伍　霞

Firefighters clear away ice from an old building in Changsha, Hunan province, on January 23, 2008.
Sanxiang Metropolitan News / Wu Xia

1月29日凌晨4时，江西九江妙庐线49号塔110千伏高压线因覆冰达100毫米而断线，九江市供电公司抢修人员在海拔1200米的雪峰激战7小时，于晚上10时修复断损线路。　淄阳晚报／顾伟东

A worker repairs a power cable tower blanketed by 100mm of ice in Jiujiang, Jiangxi province, on January 29, 2008.
Xunyang Evening News / Gu Weidong

这是湖南省湘西土家苗族自治
州龙山县电力公司的电力工人
彭勇，不顾个人安危，与同事用
长杆击冰时的情景。

湖南龙山县电力公司／田良东

Peng Yong, a worker at the
Longshan County Electric
Power Company in Xiangxi
Tujia and Miao autonomous
prefecture, Hunan province,
helps a fellow worker clear
ice from a power pole.
Hunan Longshan County Electric
Power Company / Tian Liangdong

1月25日凌晨，江西省公路局京福高速公路温沙管理处工
程队员连续工作18个小时，使路面全部疏通。通过积极组
织、科学抢险，温沙段全线在春节期间基本保证了通畅。

江西省公路局／朱益明

Workers shovel away snow on the Wensha section
of the Beijing to Fuzhou expressway in Jiangxi
province, on January 25, 2008. The expressway
resumed operation before Chinese New Year.
Jiangxi Highway Administration Bureau / Zhu Yiming

1月25日至27日，江西省抚州市临川区气象局工作人员冒着严寒在10米高空抢修自动测风仪器。　中国气象报／邹忠旺

A worker from the Linchuan Meteorological Bureau in Fuzhou, Jiangxi province, repairs an anemoscope in −10℃ temperatures, on Januray 25, 2008.　China Meteorological News / Zou Zhongwang

1月29日凌晨4时15分，江西省九江市庐山电网主动脉——110千伏妙庐线49号塔不堪冰雪重负断线，抢修人员经过近9个小时的艰难跋涉到达妙庐线抢修点，在零下10℃的恶劣条件下艰难作业。
九江日报／洪显志

Electricity workers repair damaged cables in −10℃ degree conditions. It took them nine hours to trudge through snow to reach the damaged 110,000−volt transmission tower in Jiujiang, Jiangxi province, on January 29, 2008.　Jiujiang Daily / Hong Xianzhi

江苏镇江一名警察在道路上指挥交通，他的帽子上落了一层厚厚的雪。
镇江日报／陶 春

A policeman directs traffic during heavy snowfall on a road in Zhenjiang,
Jiangsu province.　Zhenjiang Daily / Tao Chun

这是广东省韶关市乳源县洛阳镇钟屋村村民钟电强在自家菜园子里清除冰凌，
长时间冰冻使蔬菜冻死大半。　　新快报／王小明

Zhong Dianqiang of Zhongwu village in Ruyuan county, Shaoguan city,
Guangdong province, clears icicles from his vegetable garden on February 3, 2008.　　New Express / Wang Xiaoming

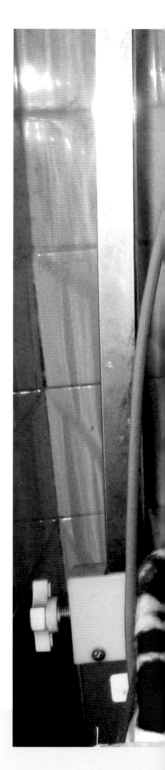

1月27日，位于安徽皖南山区的宣州区水东镇遭受连日持续强降雪。为了保证山区群众和附近工厂正常用电供应，宣城市水东供电所电工们加强了供电线路巡查和电力设备抢修，确保电力畅通。

安徽宣城金彩广告公司 / 李晓红

Electricity workers lug power equipments in heavy snow during a repair operation in the Wannan mountain area, Anhui province, January 27, 2008.

Jincai Advertising / Li Xiaohong

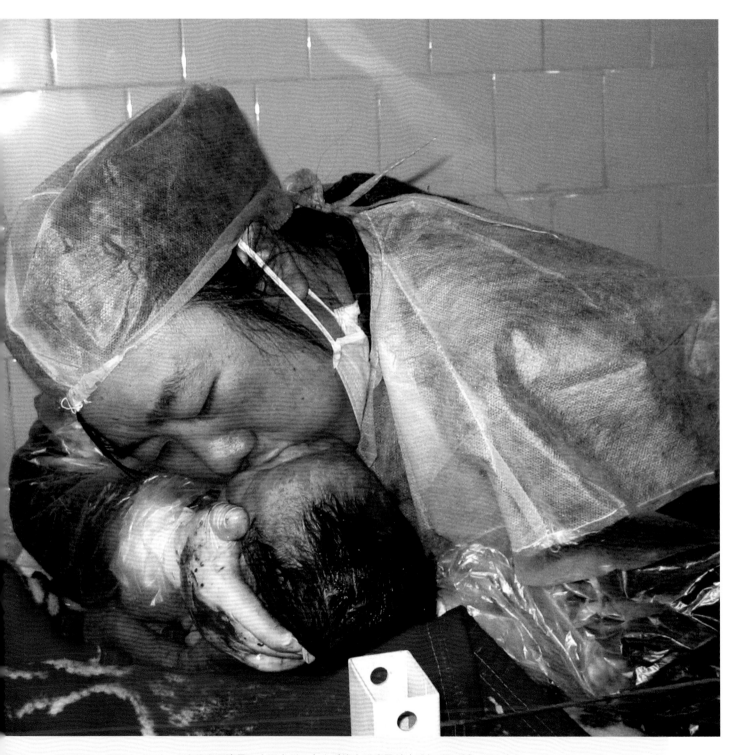

2月2日清晨，广西全州县东山瑶族乡因冰雪封冻"与世隔绝"了20多天。乡卫生院的蒋医生用嘴代替吸痰器，把男婴从死亡边缘救下来。

桂林日报／黄　政

A doctor sucks the remaining phlegm from the mouth of a newborn baby in Dongshan Yao Nationality township of Quanzhoucounty, Guangxi Zhuang autonomous region,　February 2, 2008.

Guilin Daily / Huang Zheng

2月1日，在广州火车站西侧高架桥下，解放军战士用人墙将滞留旅客隔离
分散。 华商报／张宏伟

Soldiers form a cordon to prevent people from being crushed at the
Guangzhou Railway Station, Guangdong province, February 1, 2008.
Huashang Daily / Zhang Hongwei

1月31日，广东省广州火车站广场，一位突然
昏倒的旅客被以接力传递的方式从等待进站的
人群中送出。随后，被武警官兵送到临时医疗
中心救治。　南方都市报/陈奕启

A faint woman is lifted to safety by the
crowd so that she can receive medical
treatment at the Guangzhou Railway
Station, Guangdong province, January 31,
2008.　Nanfang City News / Chen Yiqi

在浙江省杭州市下城区凤起路上，一对骑车父子艰难前行。　青年时报/张　辉

A father and his son cycle through heavy snow in Hangzhou, Zhejiang province,
February 1, 2008.　　Youth Times / Zhang Hui

抢修人员在零下10℃的恶劣条件下，拆除破损瓷瓶、修复断线。　九江日报／洪显志

A worker cuts through thick layers of ice covering a transmission tower. The temperature dropped to −10℃.　Jiujiang Daily / Hong Xianzhi

抢修人员在零下10℃的恶劣条件下，拆除破损瓷瓶、修复断线。　九江日报／洪显志

2月17日，广东佛山电视台一名记者在贵州息烽采访抢险队员时，冰雪路滑，摔倒在地。
佛山日报／赵永生

A journalist from Guangdong Foshan TV Station slips on ice during an interview in Xifeng, Guizhou province, February 17, 2008.　Foshan Daily / Zhao Yongsheng

这是法制晚报记者杨章怀随湖北通山供电公司的电工赶赴当地的凤池山抢修现场进行采访。　湖北通山供电公司／职工

This photo was taken by an unknown electricity worker and shows Yang Zhanghuai, a photographer from Legal Mirror, with electricity workers from the Hubei Tongshan Electric Power Company. Yang is climbing to a repair site on Fengchi mountain in Hubei province to interview the workers.

2月3日，为抢修湖南省郴州市开发区塘城线62号电塔，几名消防官兵抬着几百斤重的抢修用氧气瓶步行上山。图为消防官兵们正在经过半山水渠上临时搭建的"独木桥"。

南方都市报／范舟波

An oxygen cylinder is transported to workmen repairing damaged power towers in Chenzhou, Hunan province, February 3, 2008. Nanfang City News / Fan Zhoubo

2008年1月26日，为打通京珠高速公路郴州段，郴州军分区政委魏永景身先士卒，连续奋战8天8夜，昏倒在工地上。醒来之后，他又冲向工地，同战士们一起扛起两吨重的电线杆。

解放军画报／冯凯旋

Wei Yongjing, the 53-year-old commissar of the Chenzhou Military Sub-region in Hunan province, joins his soldiers to carry a 2-tonne electric pole on January 26, 2008. He was exhausted after working for eight days and nights. PLA Pictorial / Feng Kaixuan

2月18日，贵州麻洋山山顶，连日的雨雪，使本就陡峭的山路更加湿滑，战士们穿着每天被泥水打湿又无法烤干的军装，拖着裹满泥巴的双腿在山间里艰难跋涉。

解放军报／李　靖

Soldiers trudge on a muddy mountain road in Guizhou province, February 18, 2008.

PLA Daily/ Li Jing

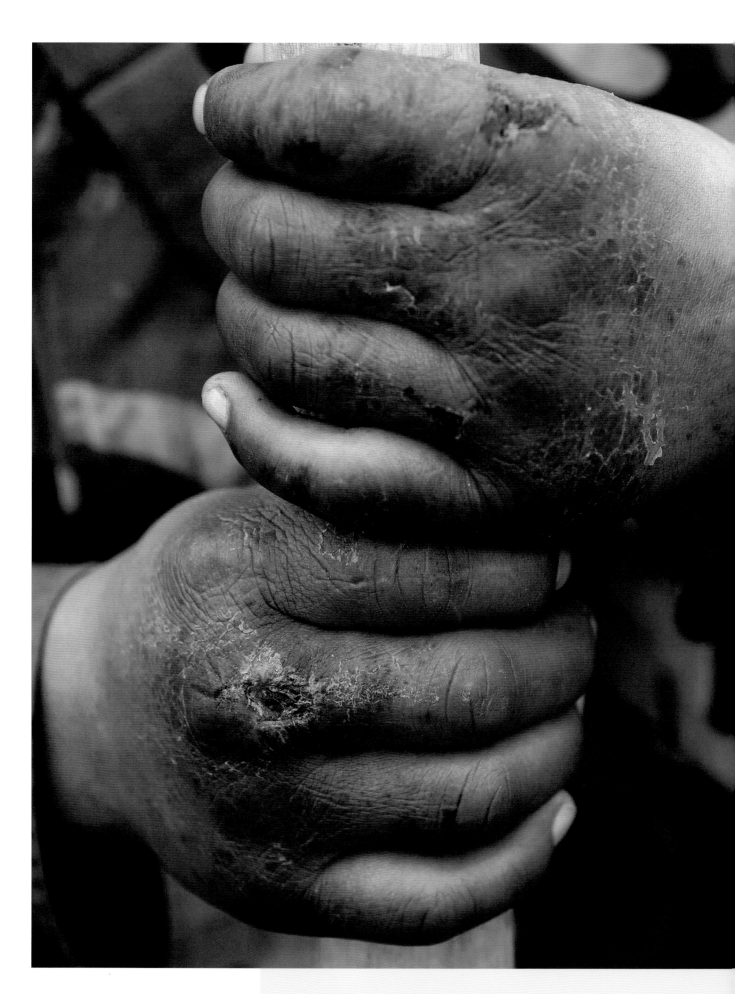

2月8日，在通往128号铁塔的山路上，一名士官因为过度劳累，不得不接受治疗。
楚天都市报／陈　勇

A soldier suffering from exhaustion is treated on a mountain road, February 8, 2008. Chutian City Express / Chen Yong

战士的手　　77100 部队／高效文

The damaged hands of a soldier who helped in the snow disaster relief.
No.77100 Troop / Gao Xiaowen

为尽快打通京珠高速大动脉，武警驻湖南某部出动了1200多名官兵，日夜奋战在京珠高速公路上，破冰铲雪，维持交通秩序。　新华社／李　刚

A soldier quenches his thirst during repair work at a section of the expressway from Beijing to Zhuhai. Military authorities sent more than 1,200 soldiers to help clear the highway.　Xinhua / Li Gang

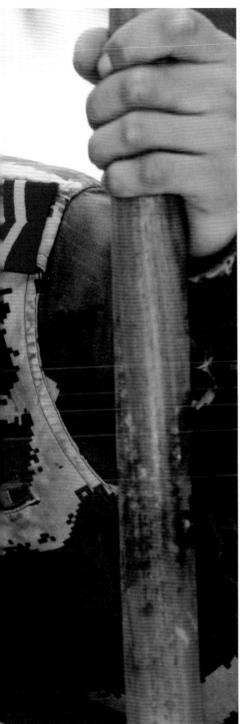

2月5日，在浙江省杭州市团委的组织下，多家企业联合组织艺术团，走进杭州市九堡镇的中国隧道建设工程公司工地，为未能按时回家过年的外来务工人员进行慰问演出。图为一位小提琴演员在纷飞的大雪中激情演奏。

杭州时报／姜胜利

A violinist performs for construction workers at a site in Jiubao town, Hangzhou city, Zhejiang province, February 5, 2008. The workers could not return to their hometowns for Chinese New Year because of the snowfall.　Hangzhou Times / Jiang Shengli

湖北省武汉市环卫部门人员正在连夜撒盐融雪。　楚天金报／刘大家

Salt is spread on icy roads to prevent accidents in Wuhan, Hubei province, January 27, 2008.
Chutian Golden Newspaper / Liu Dajia

1月30日，湖南省长沙市市民自发地组织起来，为三位牺牲在抗冰雪一线的烈士送行。
三湘都市报／于海洋

People pay their last respects to Luo Haiwen, Luo Changming and Zhou Jinghua, the electricians who died while working to restore power cut off by heavy snow in Changsha, Hunan province, on January 30, 2008. The men fell from a collapsed power pylon on January 26. They were later recognized by the provincial government as martyrs.　Sanxiang Metropolitan News / Yu Haiyang

1月30日，长沙数万人自发地为在抗冰保电中牺牲的罗海文、罗长明和周景华三位烈士送行。　长沙晚报／刘 军

Locals pay their last respects to Luo Haiwen, Luo Changming and Zhou Jinghua, the electricians who died while working to restore power supply cut off by heavy snow. The funeral was held in Changsha, Hunan province, on January 30, 2008. Changsha Evening News / Liu Jun

广西桂林受冰灾影响，电力、通信中断多日。为了保证电力、通信畅通，桂林市政府及通信公司准备了百台发电机送往各个受灾点。

广西桂林市滨江风景管理处／克　祥

Local government and telecom company staff move power generators to the snow-hit regions in Guilin, Guangxi Zhuang autonomous region.

Guangxi Guilin Binjiang Scenic Area Management Office / Ke Xiang

这是云南省镇雄县400多名职工沿着4.8公里
的输水管道燃火融冰。镇雄县委组织部/石声明

Fires are lit to thaw out a water pipe in
Zhenxiong county, Yunnan province, Feb-
ruary 16, 2008.
Organization Department of Zhenxiong County Party
Committee / Shi Shengming

2月3日凌晨，浙江省杭州市解放路丰乐桥边，一位年轻人正在救助一位被折断的大树压倒的陌生老人。　青年时报／黄伟健

A young driver stops to help an elderly man who was struck by a tree branch, which snapped under the weight of the snow in Hangzhou, Zhejiang province, February 3, 2008. Youth Times / Huang Weijian

农历除夕，湖北省输变电公司"党员突击队"奋战5天，在吃年夜饭之前将126号铁塔重新安装起来。　楚天都市报／陈　勇

Electricians from the Hubei Electric Power Company climb atop a power tower to repair damaged cables on February 6, 2008.
Chutian City Express / Chen Yong

雪天路滑，事故频发，为疏导交通，湖南岳阳地区一位女交警正在风雪中值勤。　　岳阳晚报社／范向辉

A policewoman directs traffic in Yueyang, Hunan province.　　Yueyang Evening News / Fan Xianghui

2月1日，大雪封路的武汉街头，一名搬运工正在装运煤块。　　武钢电讯公司／高战胜

A coal delivery man loads his cart in Wuhan, Hubei province, February 1, 2008.
Wuhan Steel Telecom Company / Gao Zhansheng

江苏扬州汽车站附近，一名交通巡警正在推一辆陷在雪地里的轿车。
扬州晚报／赵　军

A policeman pushes a car near a coach station in Yangzhou, Jiangsu
province.　Yangzhou Evening News / Zhao Jun

1月13日开始，受低温冰雪天气影响，上万台车辆，四五万司乘人员滞留在京珠高速公路上。　深圳晚报／汪阳

More than 10,000 vehicles and up to 50,000 passengers are stranded on an expressway linking Beijing and Zhuhai from January 13, 2008.　Shenzhen Evening News / Wang Yang

2008年春节期间，辽宁送变电工程公司抢险突击队远赴江西抗冰救灾。图为两名突击队员在江西万安境内国家电网南北向动脉"文赣线"抢修现场午间小憩。
江西万安水力发电厂／刘世彬

Two workers from Liaoning Provincial Power Transmission and Substation Project Company take a nap at a repair site in Wan'an, Jiangxi province during the Spring Festival of 2008.

Wan'an Waterpower Plant of Jiangxi province / Liu Shibin

2月1日，湖南郴州市民在罗家井农贸市场购买年货。湖南郴州遭遇近50年来最严重的冰雪灾害，全市交通运输、电力供应等遭到
极为严重的破坏，给全市人民生产、生活带来了极大的困难。郴州市政府在全力保障电力、交通、通讯的恢复和畅通的同时积极组
织调运市民生活急需的商品物资，保障市场供应。　新华社／陈树根

Local residents select and buy goods for the upcoming Spring Festival at a market in Chenzhou, Hunan province,
February 1, 2008.　Xinhua / Chen Shugen

2月6日除夕之夜，郴州市民在烛光下迎接新年的到来。 华商报／胡国庆

A girl lights firecrackers to welcome Chinese New Year in Chenzhou, Hunan province, February 6, 2008. Chenzhou went without electricity and tap water for two weeks.
Huashang Daily / Hu Guoqing

1月26日，安徽省巢湖市出现暴雪天气，给人们出行带来很大不便，道路交通受到影响。巢湖市气象台发布了暴雪和道路结冰橙色预警。
新安晚报／金学永

A man walks amid the heavy snow in Chaohu, Anhui province, January 26, 2008.
Xin'an Evening News / Jin Xueyong

重庆野生动物世界今年遇到最寒冷的冬天，为了给动物御寒，除备足了空调、取暖器、棉被等物品外，饲养员还给最怕冷的长颈鹿、犀牛等动物生火取暖。这是饲养员给长颈鹿生火取暖。　永川日报／陈仕川

Fires are lit to keep giraffes warm at a zoo in Chongqing municipality, January 29, 2008.
Yongchuan Daily / Chen Shichuan

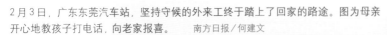

2月3日，广东东莞汽车站，坚持守候的外来工终于踏上了回家的路途。图为母亲开心地教孩子打电话，向老家报喜。　南方日报／何建文

A mother helps her daughter call their family at a coach station in Dongguan, Guangdong province on February 3, 2008. The family are about to board the bus, which will take them home.　Nanfang Daily / He Jianwen

2月3日，上海市雪后放晴，一个孩子在浦东世纪
广场国旗街玩雪。　　新闻午报／刘剑锋

National Flag Street in Shanghai on February
3，2008．　News Times / Liu Jianfeng

# 第三部分

# 真情支援

## Compassion and Care

　　灾害让我们遭遇了困难，也让我们体验了真情。全国各地心系灾区的广大军民纷纷伸出援助之手，展现出社会主义大家庭的温暖。

　　The compassion of the Chinese people shone through the snow and ice disaster and helped victims overcome their difficulties. People from all parts of the country lent a helping hand in disaster areas. Amid the cold, we felt the warmth of our large socialist family.

1月19日，中原油田油气生产一线职工克服一切困难，坚守岗位，确保油
气生产平稳运行。　　中原石油报／胡庆明

Oilfield ensure the smooth production of oil and gas, January 19,
2008.　　Zhongyuan Oil News / Hu Qingming

今年1月，江西省抚州电网遭遇有史以来最严重的冰冻灾害，驻赣武警水电
二总队主动请缨，迅速从江西、河北、山西等地输变线施工一线调集200多
名专业技术官兵火速赶到受灾现场展开紧急抢修。　　江南都市报／盛良山

Police from No.2 Hydropower Engineering Force Corps Armed Police Forces carry an electrical pole in Fuzhou, Jiangxi province in
January this year.　　Jiangnan City Daily / Sheng Liangshan

在广西桂林电缆110千伏南旺线，抢修人员在雪地中艰难寻找故障点。中新社／林希平
Repairmen walk carefully on ice-covered mountains to seek out damaged cables in Guilin, Guangxi Zhuang autonomous region.
China News Service / Lin Xiping

2月4日下午，广州火车站内，在战士们的有序疏导下，广州火车站的滞留旅客得到了有效疏散。四名疲惫的战士在连续执勤39个小时后和部队的其他战士一起换防休息，因过度疲惫靠着铁栅栏站着就睡着了。　　广州日报/邵权达

Four soldiers doze off after working 39-hours straight helping the stranded passengers at the Guangzhou Railway Station, Guangdong province, February 4, 2008.　　Guangzhou Daily / Shao Quanda

2月23日，郴州电力员工及郴州市民为唐山13位农民自发组成的"义务救灾小分队"送行。　郴州日报／李细万

Thirteen farmers from Tangshan, Hebei province, who voluntarily joined the snow disaster relief effort in Chenzhou, Hunan province, saluet to Chenzhou's citizens before they go back home on February 23, 2008.　Chenzhou Daily / Li Xiwan

2月5日，湖南省湘乡市壶天镇，前来支援的甘肃送变电工程公司的250名职工自带方便面上山抢修供电铁塔。　武汉晚报／周国强

Armed with boxes of instant noodles, workers from an electric power company of Gansu province make their way to Hutian town, Hunan province, to help restore power supplies, on February 5, 2008.
Wuhan Evening News / Zhou Guoqiang

2月18日，江西省永新县石桥镇北岭村村民们提着鸡蛋、花生等，自发地为圆满完成任务后"转移战场"的南京军区空军某部官兵送行。　南京军区空军宣传处／贲道春

Local villagers offer eggs to soldiers at a military base in Nanjing of Jiangsu province in appreciation for their relief work in Yongxin county, Jiangxi province, February 18, 2008.

Propaganda Department of Nanjing Air Force / Ben Daochun

因冰雪灾害，邮政交通受到严重影响，邮政职工坚持以步代车送邮件。图为湖南省一名邮递员正冒着大雪步行投送邮件。　中新社／桂志强

A postwoman delivers mails on foot in heavy snow in Hunan province.
*China News Service / Gui Zhiqiang*

1月25日，受路面结冰影响，京珠高速公路上滞留了一万多辆车，高速交警联合地方政府开展大救援行动。图为高速交警正在京珠高速公路长潭段给被困司机免费发放食物。

湖南省交警总队高速公路管理支队新闻工作室／章　尧

Stranded motorists, mostly truck drivers, reach out for food packets offered by policemen on the Changtan section of the expressway from Beijing to Zhuhai in Hunan province, January 25, 2008.

Newsroom of Highway Management　Division , Hunan Traffic Police Troop / Zhang Yao

河南郑州铁路局新密车站调车组人员正在冒着大雪编组车辆。

郑州市宋寨火车站／司向东

A worker from the Songzhai Railway Station in Zhengzhou, Henan province, is busy arranging train schedules.

Songzhai Railway Station / Si Xiangdong

滞留在长沙的宋静、宋家乐姐弟俩终于高兴地坐上第一批
"绿丝带"爱心车。　三湘都市报／田　超

Song Jiale and his sister Song Jing are driven to
their hometown of Xiangtan by a local citzen after
they were stranded in Changsha, Hunan province.
Sanxiang Metropolitan News / Tian Chao

深夜，广州空军运输航空兵某团近四百名官兵正在抢装运往受灾地区的救援物资。
广州空军政治部／沈　玲

Bundles of quilts are loaded onto plane bound for the disaster—hit areas. Nearly 400 soldiers from
Guangzhou Air Force were organized to dispatch disaster-relief materials.
Political Department of Guangzhou Air Force / Shen Ling

为保证蔬菜供应，湖北省武汉市某无公害蔬菜基地组织近五千菜农，用扁担、三轮车将各种蔬菜送到交易点。　　长江日报／张　宁

About 5,000 farmers carry and cycle vegetables to a market by shoulder poles and tricycles in Wuhan, Hubei province, January 27, 2008. *Yangtze River Daily / Zhang Ning*

2月5日，安徽省霍邱县灾区群众领到了中央宣传部和国家广电总局为受灾农民捐助的收音机。
霍邱县委宣传部／王兴远

Contact with the outside world is established once again after residents in Huoqiu county, Anhui province, receive radios provided by the Propaganda Department of the CPC Central Committee and the State Administration of Radio, Film and Television, on February 5, 2008.
Propaganda Department of Huoqiu County Party Committee ／ Wang Xingyuan

春节期间，开滦集团要求下属10多个生产矿井的矿工们全部坚持生产。大年初一，开滦唐山矿业公司的矿工们刚一上井就吃上了公司特意为他们准备的饺子。　　开滦日报／石　宁

Miners enjoy traditional Spring Festival dumplings in Kailuan, Hebei province on February 7, 2008. Workers from more than 10 coal fields, operated by the Kailuan Group, worked during the Spring Festival. 　Kailuan Daily ／ Shi Ning

2月3日，成都军区6架直升机将棉被等御寒物资空运到四川省宜宾市的兴文县、宜宾县、长宁县等受灾严重地区。　成都晚报／杨

A military helicopter transports disaster-relief materials to snow-hit counties in Yibin, Sichuan province, February 3, 2008.　Chengdu Evening News / Li Yang

第四部分

# 重建家园

## Rebuilding Our Home

　　灾害让我们经受了考验，更让我们展示了力量。面对灾后重建的繁重任务，我们振奋精神，团结奋战，自强不息。冰雪过后的大地已经再现活力，重建家园的脚步声正响在我们耳畔。

　　The snow and ice disaster was an ordeal, but it revealed the strength of the human spirit. With a unified spirit, we struggled together and continuously strived to rebuild our lives after the disaster.

2月16日，"硬骨头六连"在江西省永新县石桥镇岩崖山抢修通往井冈山电网的工
地上。　　解放军报／乔天富

Soldiers carry electrical poles to the top of a hill where electricity towers
were damaged by snow disaster in Yongxin county, Jiangxi province,
February 16, 2008.　　PLA Daily / Qiao Tianfu

2月19日，援粤抗冰的安徽省电力公司从广西紧急调来一队马帮，支援广东韶关灾后重建±500千伏江城输电线路的抗灾运输工作。　安徽省淮北供电公司／王　文

Horses carry materials to help repair an electrical pylon, which was damaged during snowfalls, in Shaoguan, Guangdong province, February 19, 2008.
Huaibei Electric Power Company ／ Wang Wen

一名参加贵州电网重建的电力工人正在检查坠地导线。
新京报／郭铁流

An electrician checks an electricity cable in Guizhou province.　The Beijing News / Guo Tieliu

2月5日，成都铁路局调集车皮，紧急装运四川省电力公司支援湖南灾区的2000多吨31车的电杆、电缆、变压器等电力设备，支援灾区人民重建家园。
西南铁道报／曹　宁

Electricity poles, cables and power generators, weighing more than 2,000 tons, are loaded on train carriages in Chengdu, Sichuan province, February 5, 2008. The materials are bound for Hunan province.　Southwest Railway News / Cao Ning

在江西上栗县，当地工人与陕西电力公司救援队抓紧灾后抢修，确保省政府提出的
3月6日通电目标。　江西萍乡市宣传科／周建林

Workers fix a transformer substation tower, which was damaged during
snowfalls in Shangli county, Jiangxi province, to ensure that the electrical
power supply can be resumed before March 6, 2008.
Propaganda Department of Pingxiang City Party Committee / Zhou Jianlin

2月11日，在湖南省郴州市城前岭500万千伏电塔抢修现场，来自河南的电力工人们肩扛手提地把电线杆送上山头。　郴州市摄影家协会／周建生

Workers from Henan province, carry electrical poles to the top of a hill, where a 500,000-volt transmission tower was damaged during snowfall in Chenzhou, Hunan province, February 11, 2008.　Chenzhou Photographers Association / Zhou Jiansheng

几名夜班工人正在连夜焊接电线杆龙骨。
新京报／郭铁流

Workers who are on duty in the nights weld
telegraph poles.    The Beijing News / Guo Tieliu

1月中旬，驻浙某部万名官兵火速赶赴江西赣州抢险，帮助当地运送电塔器材，恢复生产生活用电。图为
战士们用肩膀将七八百斤重的电塔设备运到陡峭的山头。    钱江晚报／林云龙

Soldiers from Zhejiang province heave a 400-kilogram piece of equipment to a mountain site in
Ganzhou, Jiangxi province in the middle of January, 2008.
Qianjiang Evening News / Lin Yunlong

1月31日，共青团黑龙江省委组织开展"团组织关爱留守的少先队员春风行动"，向留守的少先队员发放了电话卡，让留守学生与在外打工的父母通话。这是哈尔滨市平房区平新镇平乐小学五年级一班12岁的鞠英楠，眼含热泪给远在湖南长沙打工的父亲通电话。　哈尔滨日报／刘　洋

Twelve-year-old Harbin student Ju Yingnan calls her father, who is stranded in Changsha in Hunan province. A local Harbin organization provided free phone cards for migrant workers' children in Harbin, Heilongjiang province, January 31, 2008.　Harbin Daily / Liu Yang

为了让山村人民在春节期间用上电，浙江省龙泉市电力局在节前组织力量抢修损坏的线路。图为农历腊月二十九，电力工人在屏南镇塘山村抢修线路。
浙江省龙泉市中等职业学校／潘世国

Workers from the Longquan Electric Power Bureau carry an electrical pole to fix broken lines in Pingnan town, Zhejiang province, February 5, 2008. Longquan Secondary Vocational School / Pan Shiguo

吴菊兰，是兴国县民兵应急电力抢修分队民兵姜景旺的新娘；蔡满兰，是驻京某部士官刘庆的新娘。
春节期间，两对新人一起坚守在保电第一线。2月19日上午，两位新娘给抢修电网的民兵们送来姜汤，
战友们趁机在电网抢修现场，为两对新人办了一场特殊的婚礼。　　　上海警备区政治部宣传处/陈鸿亮

A wedding ceremony is held for two soldiers and their brides on February 19, 2008.
The soldiers postponed their wedding plans to fight for the snow disaster.
Propaganda Department of Shanghai Garrison Command / Chen Hongliang

2月2日，随着春节临近，湖南省郴州市街头开始出现挑着节日饰品的小贩。
北京青年报/袁　艺

Despite heavy snow, the spirit of Chinese New Year lived on. This
vendor peddled her wares, which included the symbols of happiness
in Chenzhou, Hunan province, February 2, 2008.
Beijing Youth Daily / Yuan Yi

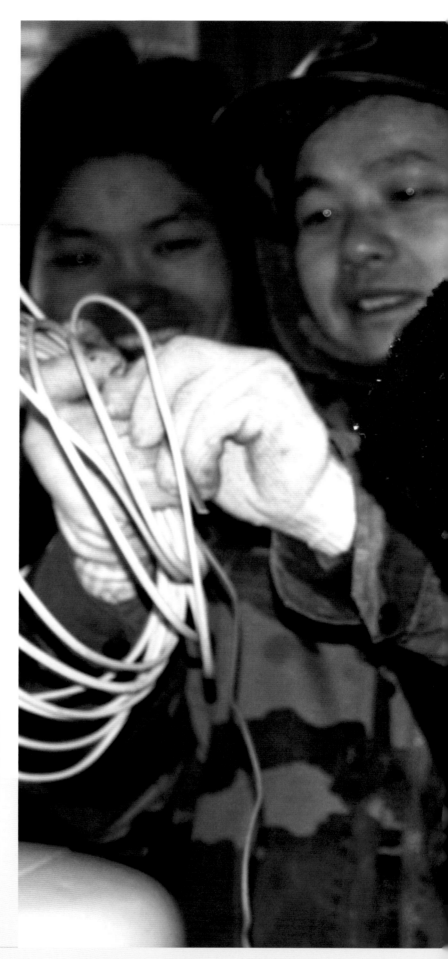

1月中旬以来，湖南邵阳县遭遇历史罕见的冰灾，15个电信交换点线路中断，近两万台有线电话无法使用。经过全县200多名电信职工的奋力抢修，2月1日，中断20天的电话终于修通了。图为邵阳县红星村村民彭美照在与亲友通电话。　　湖南省邵阳县下花桥镇通讯组／李爱民

Peng Meizhao calls his family after telephone connections were restored in his Hongxing village, in Shaoyang county, Hunan province, February 1, 2008. Fifteen telecom base stations were damaged affecting 20,000 telephones.
Communication Department of Xiahuaqiao Town Party Committee / Li Aimin

2月15日，南京军区某部官兵在江西九江武宁县罗溪乡海拔960多米的南山抢运损毁铁塔所需主材。　江西日报／燕　平

Soldiers based in Nanjing of Jiangsu province move poles onto Nanshan mountain in Luoxi village, Jiangxi province, February 15, 2008.　Jiangxi Daily / Yan Ping

2月2日，桂林市灵川县海洋乡，当地移动通信公司的维修工正在向海拔800米处的通信线路抢修现场搬运器材。　广西桂林市兴东方律师事务所／郑　法

A worker from local mobile communication company carries equipments to a repair site in Lingchuan county, Guilin city, Guangxi Zhuang autonomous region, February 2, 2008.　Xingdongfang Law Office / Zheng Fa

2月19日7时15分，经过10天的抢修，停电达23天之久的江西省宜黄县终于通电了。凤岗镇河东村郑思成等几位村民欢呼雀跃。据悉，受雪灾的影响，宜黄县是全国最后一个恢复通电的县。
江南日报／梁振堂

Local villagers celebrate when the power resumed in Yihuang county, Jiangxi province, after a 23-day blackout. Yihuang county was the last county in China to have its power supply switched back on.    *Jiangnan Daily / Liang Zhentang*

# 结 束 语

## Show of strength and spirit

2008年，我们彰显了抗击雨雪冰冻灾害的无穷力量。事实再一次证明，只要紧紧依靠广大人民群众，充分发挥社会主义制度能够集中力量办大事的政治优势，我们就一定能够战胜前进道路上的各种挑战和风险，不断把中国特色社会主义伟大事业推向前进。

Our great strength and spirit, in the face of adversity, rose to new heights during the snow disaster in 2008. Our efforts proved once again we are able to overcome any challenge on the road ahead. The disaster showed we can constantly push forward our great cause of building socialism with. Chinese characteristics, as long as we closely rely on the broad masses of the people, While giving full play to the advantages of socialist political system, in concentrating forces on major tasks.

**图书在版编目（CIP）数据**

抗击冰雪 心系人民：新闻摄影展作品集：汉、英／
鞠鹏等摄．—北京：人民美术出版社，2008.5
　ISBN 978-7-102-04236-7

　Ⅰ.抗… Ⅱ.鞠… Ⅲ.新闻摄影—中国—现代—摄影集
Ⅳ.J429.1

中国版本图书馆 CIP 数据核字（2008）第 043233 号

# 抗击冰雪　心系人民
### 新闻摄影展作品集

编辑出版　人民美术出版社
　　　　　（100735　北京北总布胡同 32 号）
　　　　　电　话　65253173　65122617
　　　　　http://www.renmei.com.cn

责任编辑　李　翎
版式设计　袁　毅
责任校对　江金照　朱　布
责任印制　丁宝秀
制版印刷　北京雅昌彩色印刷有限公司
经　　销　新华书店总店北京发行所

2008 年 5 月　第 1 版　第 1 次印刷
开本：889 毫米×1194 毫米　1/16　印张：7
印数：0001-5200 册
定价：60.00 元